DANCE OF LOVE

A MINNESOTA LAKES ROMANCE

ROSE MARIE

A MINNESOTA FESTIVAL ROMANCE

DANCE OF LOVE

BY

ROSE MARIE MEUWISSEN

Dance of Love
by
Rose Marie Meuwissen

Dance of Love
Digital/Print Edition
Copyright 2016 by Rose Marie Meuwissen
https://www.rosemariemeuwissen.com

NO GHOSTWRITERS WERE USED IN THE CREATION OF THIS BOOK. THIS WORK OF FICTION IS 100% THE ORIGINAL WORK OF ROSE MARIE MEUWISSEN.

Print ISBN- 978-1-954030-91-6
Published in the United States of America
Nordic Publishing
Edited by Sherri Hildebrandt
Cover Design by Rose Marie Meuwissen

❀ Created with Vellum

A MINNESOTA FESTIVAL ROMANCE

RENAISSANCE FESTIVAL

Sarina never imagined by dancing with her Belly Dancing 101 class on the stage at the Renaissance Festival, she would meet Tony, one undeniably hot and sexy Italian stud. But after ditching him at the front gate, would she be able to dance her way back into his heart?

When Tony watched Sarina walk away from him without even a chance to get her phone number, he never expected to see her again. Apparently, fate had other plans.

A MINNESOTA FESTIVAL ROMANCE

MINNESOTA

Land of Many Festivals

DEDICATION

TO A FRIEND WHO WAS A HOUSEWIFE AND
MOTHER, BUT ALSO WAS AN EXCELLENT
'BELLY DANCER'.

CHAPTER 1

*H*ips swaying to the beat of the music, their bodies moved in unison. Multitudes of shiny coins jangled melodically from where they were attached to the colorful hip scarves neatly tied below their waists revealing flat stomachs. Sarina was one of several ladies lined up in front of the mirror at the dance studio where she and her best friends, Kelsey and Dana, practiced their dance routine in their Belly Dancing 101 class.

"Looks good, ladies." The instructor complimented the class. "I think you're ready for our performance on Saturday night at the Renaissance Festival."

"I don't know about this, I took the class for exercise and fun. Not to perform," Sarina said.

"What's the matter with you? This will be fun!" Dana answered.

"Maybe for you. I just don't know if I feel comfortable dancing in front of people, strangers actually, and basically being half naked." Sabrina waived her hands over her scarcely covered breasts and bare stomach.

"That's the best part. We won't know any of them!" Kelsey added with total enthusiasm.

"You guys are crazy exhibitionists!" Sarina stated emphatically.

"Yes, but you're going to join us in this little adventure, aren't you?" Dana pleaded with hands on hips.

"Please," Kelsey added, giving her best pouty face.

"I just know I'm going to regret this, but yes, I'll do it," Sarina finally said after going over all the reasons she shouldn't do it in her head. "All I have to say is there'd better not be anyone there I know."

"My place tomorrow after work, say six o'clock?" Dana asked.

"We can try on and model our shiny new costumes," Kelsey stated.

"You got yours, didn't you, Sarina?" Dana asked.

Sarina contemplated saying no. Then she wouldn't have to be a part of the performance, but finally answered. "Yes, but now I'm wishing I hadn't."

Sarina, Dana and Kelsey parked in the massive parking lot, aka farmer's field, in a spot at least a half mile away from the Renaissance Festival front gate.

"We'll be exhausted by the time we get to the gate," Kelsey said as they walked toward the entrance carrying the garment bags containing their shimmering new belly dancing costumes.

"Yeah, I don't see why we didn't get VIP parking passes since we are performing free for the festival," Dana added.

"Well, at least we got passes to get in free," Sarina said as she handed one to the ticket taker, dressed in his medieval beggar costume, who was leering at them.

"What you got in the bags, Ladies," he asked gruffly.

Sarina started to say, "None of your business," but was cut off by Dana.

"We're belly dancers in the belly dancing show today." Dana smiled seductively and swayed her hips as the ticket taker's eyes took in her sexy body. He waved them through the gate.

"I don't believe you just did that!" Sarina said more sternly than she intended.

"Lighten up, she's excited. Let's go check in." Kelsey motioned towards the medieval castle ahead where they were doing the show.

"Who knows maybe we'll meet some really hot guys today!" Dana exclaimed.

Sarina couldn't believe she was doing this. She didn't like talking in front of people much less dancing. Her palms were sweating, and her heart was beating rapidly in her chest. Adjusting her teal green, fitted top that looked more like a super fancy, beaded up bra, she noticed how it made her green eyes stand out. After the silk scarf with all the dangling coins was tied around her hips over the beautiful, teal, billowy pants, she put the final touches on her silky long black hair falling in loose curls over her shoulders and down her back. Gazing into the mirror to be sure her make-up was just perfect, she backed up a couple steps to take a look at herself in the full length mirror. She liked what she saw. There actually was a sexy hot woman staring back at her, who looked way more confident than she felt.

"Ready?" Dana asked. "They're lining up."

Sarina followed Dana to the side of the stage where Kelsey and the other seven women from their class along with their teacher were already in line. She wasn't so sure she could do this. Maybe she could just tell them she didn't feel well and would need to sit out the performance back stage. But while she was mulling over her options, she found herself following the others out onto the stage. She looked out at the massive audience of medieval costumed men and women, and sheer terror gripped her body. Could she really do this?

$\mathcal{T}$ony Sorelli took another gulp of some of the nastiest tasting ale he'd ever tasted. The meal served to the attendees was only mediocre as far as he was concerned, so he wasn't expecting much from the show, either. At least they were in the front row, so they would have a great view of the dancers. He was only there because his two buddies, John Danfield and Brad Davis, from college were in town from California for the weekend and had insisted on going to the Renaissance Festival held in Shakopee every year from mid-August to the first week of October. For old time's sake. While attending college some ten years ago, they'd had a ritual of attending the festival as many weekends as possible. They'd drink and eat to their heart's desire, watch as many shows as they could fit in and then, when they could barely stand up any longer, call for a cab. Young and stupid is what they'd been.

Now they were older, more mature, and had great jobs, so what were they doing here? To think in college, they'd considered themselves such cool dudes on the prowl trying to pick up women at the festival. It had never worked out well back then. He couldn't believe they were even thinking about trying it again now.

"Take a look at those babes," Brad said, pointing to the stage.

"Wow!" John said staring at the stage in disbelief. "Those women are smoking hot!"

Finally Tony took another swig of his ale and glanced toward the stage. There he saw an extremely beautiful woman dancing directly in front of him. Her exotic features spoke of a Greek heritage. At least that would be his guess. Her long, flowing, black hair framed her face, and the teal belly dancing costume fit her body perfectly. At least the covered parts, anyway. His eyes locked with her green eyes for a moment as her body flowed in rhythm with the music. He was mesmerized by her beauty. He couldn't look away.

What was the matter with him? He was single, but picking up women, much less a belly dancer wasn't his style at all. Besides he had a reputation to uphold. After all, he was a small business owner of his own roofing company. It had been his dad's, who was now retired, and was a business he'd worked in since he was a teenager.

The dancers finished and exited the stage as he continued watching them.

"Let's go meet the dancers," he heard himself say. He knew he hadn't had too much to drink, but still it was affecting his judgement and obviously his actions. They proceeded to the exit and waited by the rear stage door.

"You're all right, man," Brad said patting him on the back.

The women filed out, not dressed in the sheer, revealing costumes any longer but in skin tight jeans and sexy low cut tops. It made no difference what she wore, he would recognize those piercing green eyes anywhere. Although, he had no idea what he was going to say to her once she was standing in front of him. But it didn't matter because Brad initiated a conversation immediately with one of her friends and invited the three women to join them.

"I'm Tony," he said extending his hand to her.

"Sarina," she answered shaking his hand.

The others introduced themselves, and before he knew it they'd started to walk down the weaving paths of the festival as the delicious aromas of festival foods wafted through the air.

"I was absolutely mesmerized by your dancing," he said to Sarina. He sensed she was a bit uneasy, but could feel the attraction between them and hoped she could also.

"Thank you," she answered. "It was my first time dancing in public, and I was extremely nervous."

"I didn't notice," he said. "You ladies definitely looked like you knew what you were doing."

They walked down the well-worn dirt paths filled with food vendors and retail shops selling everything from candles to paintings to jewelry. Tony had no idea they were walking toward the exit until they reached it.

"Would you ladies like sit down and have a drink?" Tony asked trying to keep the conversation moving along. He had a feeling the dancers were planning on leaving. Boy, he must've really lost his touch with women!

"I have to get going, it was nice to meet you guys," Sarina said taking a few steps backwards before waving good-bye and heading toward the parking lot to find her car. The other women said their good-byes reluctantly and followed her, as she apparently was the driver.

"We just got ditched," Tony said, stating the obvious as they watched the women walk away.

CHAPTER 3

"Sarina, you're no fun," Dana said as they walked to the car.

"I know, but we're too old to get picked up at the Renaissance Festival by some strange men we know nothing about. Hell, we're almost thirty! Way too old for this kind of stuff."

"They were hot. Had a bit much to drink, but hot," Kelsey added.

"I think that Tony guy was interested in you, Sarina," Dana said.

"He did mention he liked my dancing, but he's a guy and guys naturally would get turned on by a belly dancing show."

"Well, we hoped to meet some guys, and we did. Didn't you think Tony was hot?" Kelsey asked.

"Sure, I guess so. He was tall, dark and handsome. Probably Italian with a name like Tony. And he seemed to have bit of an arrogant appearance about him. But I'm sure I'll never see him again, so what does it matter?" Sarina said, feeling absolutely sure what she was saying was true.

Mondays always were hectic days at the Fidelity Bank where Sarina worked as a loan officer, and today was no different. The day was long and she had one more loan applicant to see before her day was done.

She walked up to the receptionist desk to get the last person's name so she could try to help them get a loan.

"Anthony Sorelli?" she said to the back of the gentleman sitting in the reception area. She watched him stand and face her. Instantly, she recognized him.

He extended his hand to shake hers, "I go by Tony." His eyes lit up.

"Sarina Sarcova," she answered shaking his hand and hoping he didn't remember her although from the smirk on his face, she was sure he did. "This way." She walked to her office and he followed her. "Please take a seat." She motioned to the chair at her desk and he sat down.

"What can I help you with, Tony?" she asked sitting down in her chair and facing him, trying not to show how nervous she felt about seeing him again.

"I'm looking for a new pick-up truck for my business and need an auto loan. Gotta say this is a little awkward." He kept his eyes on her the whole time.

"Sorry, I'm the only loan officer still here tonight. If you want to come back tomorrow, I can have someone else help you," she offered, hoping he'd take her up on it.

"No, that's okay. I don't have anything to hide, and I'm sure you have to keep everything confidential, right?" he asked.

She nodded.

"Okay, let me take a look at the application." She quickly scanned over it and plugged everything into the computer loan application system. Nowadays everything was computerized, so within minutes she had an approval. "Looks like the system approved you. So we just need to see the income verification and the purchase agreement from the dealership where you are buying the truck. Then we can drop the money in your checking account and you can write the dealership a check."

Her nerves were obviously getting the best of her. She was an experienced loan officer and knew her job well. His credit report was exceptional, and his income was high. But he was so hot her hands were shaking! He probably wasn't interested in her at all. Why was she even thinking about this?

"Thanks," he said. "I'll have the dealership send over the documentation after we agree on the specific truck and sale price." He stood up and flashed her a smile. "I guess I need your phone number."

"Oh, yes. Here is my business card with my phone number and email." She handed him her card.

"Mind if I call you?" he asked.

Her heart was pounding rapidly in her chest and she felt totally flustered. What was she supposed to say? "Do you mean me personally?"

"Yes. You intrigue me." He waited patiently for her answer, never breaking eye contact.

"Sorry, I make it a habit of not mixing my business and personal lives." She showed him to the door.

"I understand totally, but I'm thinking it's a mistake this time. Just for the record, you looked really hot in the belly dancing costume." He left without turning back.

Sarina walked back into her office and sat down at her desk. She'd made the right decision, hadn't she? He was extremely handsome, about six feet tall, totally buff, and a business man. They definitely had chemistry! The attraction between them was strong, but that only meant the sex would be really good. Besides she may never see him again. So did it really matter at all?

Tony was pissed to say the least. Sarina had shut him down for a second time! And he wasn't totally sure why. She was a beautiful woman, and he was definitely attracted to her physically. He was sure the sex would be hot and mind-blowing. Unfortunately, he most likely wouldn't get to find out. Had he come on too strong? Not that he was aware of. He'd only asked if he could call her, because he really wanted to take her out so they could get to know each other. To see if there was more to this than the physical attraction.

It appeared the connection between them was not to be. Unfortunately, he couldn't erase the picture in his mind of Sarina's sparkling green eyes and the curves of her sensuous body in the belly dancing costume. But most of all, the feeling of defeat wasn't something he was used to.

Thank God for the internet. He was able to finish up the loan for his pick-up truck via the dealer who took care of the paperwork by emailing Sarina the purchase agreement. So much for Sarina. He hadn't needed to call her for anything else regarding the loan and had no plans to call her in the future for any other reason. The business card in his hand was soon ripped in half and in the garbage.

CHAPTER 4

"Sarina! Wasn't sure you were going to make it," Dana said to her as she walked into the dance studio for their weekly class.

"Why wouldn't I?" she asked, not sure why Dana thought she wasn't coming.

"Thought you might be out on a date with the hot guy from the Renaissance Festival." Kelsey teased her with a wide, expectant grin.

Sarina baited her friends with a tease of her own. "I did talk to him."

"I knew he'd call you. But wait, how did he get your number?" Dana questioned.

"He came into the bank, my bank, by sheer accident to get a loan."

"O.M.G! Are you serious?" Kelsey asked.

"Totally!" Sarina assured.

"So give! What happened? Did he ask you out?" Kelsey asked as they walked into the practice room.

"I gave him my business card, because it's part of my job. But…" Sarina started to answer before she was cut off.

"So he called you then?" Dana could barely control her excitement.

"No, I told him the phone number was purely for business. So I haven't heard from him since that day." Sarina continued changing into her leggings and sport bra. She couldn't help thinking about Tony. His chiseled face with those deep chestnut brown eyes haunted her, along with his broad chest and muscled arms. He looked damn good in the tight jeans he'd worn at the Renaissance Festival and equally good in his business attire at the bank. She really did want a chance to get to know him, especially after she'd realized he was a respected business man and not some scum bag guy who was just out picking up women at local festivals.

A few minutes later she and her friends were in the dance studio practicing the 'Turkish Figure Eight,' a movement of the hips moving in opposite directions. As one hip moved forward, away from the body and the back, and then the back to center; the other hip moved back, into the center, forward, and then away from the body. Sarina had this movement down and her body flowed fluidly in rhythm to the music. Next they practiced the 'Zar Head' movement where she rotated her head in circles, swirling her long hair into the air.

Today, she felt sexy as she watched herself in the mirror. She wondered what it would be like to give a private dance to a man she was interested in and if the sex afterwards would be great. She always felt aroused after dancing, but why was she having these thoughts? Was it all because of Tony?

The hour-long class flew by, and before she knew it, they were finished and leaving the studio.

"Don't forget we're going to the Mediterranean Cruise restaurant to have dinner and watch the show with our class on Friday night," Dana reminded them.

"I can't wait to watch Madeline dancing!" Kelsey added.

"I'll be there. We're meeting at six thirty, right?" Sarina asked.

"Yes, see you Friday," Dana said.

Sarina got into her car. She'd almost forgotten about Friday night. The class had been talking about it for weeks. They were going to watch their instructor, Madeline, dance in the show at the only local restaurant where Mediterranean cuisine was served and also offered a belly dancing show: The Mediterranean Cruise in Burnsville.

Matt stopped by Roofs by Design on his way home from work on Friday. Tony's shiny new pick-up was still parked outside the building so he walked in. "Tony, you still up for having a couple drinks tonight?"

Tony looked up from his desk and closed the file folder he'd been looking at to see his best friend. It had been a long day, and he was tired and really didn't feel like going out, but since he'd said he would, and Matt was standing in front of him, he was positive there was no way of getting out of it. "Sure. Your timing is great. Just finished up here."

"Kyle thought we should go to that Mediterranean Cruise place in Burnsville. It's the only place where we can get a chance to see some belly dancing action. We know you, John, and Brad already saw them at the Renaissance, but we need to check it out and see what's got you so hot and bothered. Maybe this time we'll all get lucky and get some phone numbers," Matt said as they walked out of the office.

"Not likely, but hey if you guys want to check it out, let's go," Tony said and got into his truck. He put the window down. "I'll meet you there."

"Like the truck, Tony," Matt said as got into his truck and drove out of the parking lot.

Kyle was already seated at a table up front with a full view of the stage. They joined him at the table in the quickly filling room and almost immediately were handed menus by a sexy hostess. Tony did a quick once over of the room. It was a practice he'd learned from his dad who was in the military. You always needed to know your surroundings, the people around you and your exits. Not that he'd ever needed to use any of it; it was just a habit.

They ordered drinks and food, while talking about how their past week had gone.

"Can't believe she was your loan officer! What are the chances of that happening?" Kyle asked in disbelief.

"Extremely slim I imagine," Tony said.

"And she turned you down flat twice? That must be a record for you!" Matt said.

"Just keeping it on a professional level for her job," Tony said, more to make himself believe it than Matt.

"Right." Kyle sounded as if he didn't believe a word he'd just said.

"No is no, man," Matt said as the waitress brought their food.

"Right, so I'll be moving on to the next one. End of discussion," Tony stated and they began eating.

He was in the process of making a huge effort to remove Sarina from his mind, when she walked in and sat down at a table on the other side of the stage with a group of women. What were the odds he would run into her again? Extremely slim, he would've predicted. Thankfully, she was in the audience, which he sincerely hoped meant she wasn't going to be one of the belly dancers tonight in the show. He wasn't sure he could watch her sexy body dancing on the stage tonight.

He had control of his desires, but just looking at her was arousing him and she was only sitting at the table. Maybe she wouldn't notice him, and since the guys didn't know what she looked like, there was a chance he could make it through the night with no one the wiser.

CHAPTER 5

*S*arina walked into the Mediterranean Cruise and spotted her classmates at a table up front by the stage. They were already drinking wine and having a lively conversation when she sat down. Everyone was excited to watch Madeline perform. The waitress took their food orders, and Sarina ordered a glass of Merlot.

The lights dimmed and the billowing black stage curtains opened. Three belly dancers began methodically moving to the beat of the music. She watched in awe as Madeline and her two friends filled the room with their sexual allure. It oozed from their scantily clad bodies swaying in all the moves they'd taught their students in the Belly Dancing 101 class. Sarina had to admit she needed a lot more practice after watching the professionals perform. They were damn good!

Madeline and her friends joined them at their table after the show, still dressed in their costumes. Madeline's was a deep burgundy, her friends were dressed in dark forest green and deep royal blue. Their skin glowed from spray tans and glistened from spray on glitter. They looked sexy and beautiful.

"You guys were absolutely awesome," Kelsey said.

"Incredible," Dana added. "I'll never be that good."

"It just takes time and lots of practice. You can get there if you want to," Madeline told her.

A few minutes later Sarina walked to the ladies' restroom, and when she was exiting bumped into a man probably on his way to the men's restroom.

"Excuse me, I'm so sorry," Sarina said, and when she turned to look at him, she stared into sexy brown eyes. "Tony?"

"Sarina," Tony said.

She slowly regained her composure even though she could feel an all-consuming desire deep inside her from the mere touch of his chest against hers, as a flush of heat flowed through her body. "What are you doing here?" She hoped he wasn't stalking her. But then again she was beginning to have a change of heart. Maybe it wouldn't be such a bad thing to have him pursue her.

"Just here with the guys. Told them about the belly dancing show at the Renaissance Festival, and they thought it would be fun to check one out, so here we are."

"Oh, well it's nice to see you again. You got your new truck—I mean I saw the paperwork came through."

"Yes, the whole process went very smoothly. Thank you," he said. "Well, I'll let you get back to your friends." And then he walked away toward the men's restroom.

"We saw you talking to a guy. That was him, right?" Dana asked excitedly, when she got back to the table.

"Yes, that was him," Sarina answered.

"Well, what did he say?" Kelsey chimed in.

"Nothing, he just happens to be here with some of his friends. I accidentally bumped into him on my way back, so don't go getting all excited and making something out of nothing."

"Okay," Dana said. "Let's change the subject."

"Yes, so what's going on tomorrow?" Kelsey asked.

"We're going to Emma's Krumbee's Apple Orchard, remember?" Dana said. "It'll be great. Afterwards let's try making some apple pies."

"Sounds like fun. I've never made one before," Sarina said, her mind totally on Tony not apples.

"Never?" Dana asked.

"My mom was a perfectionist when it came to making pies, so she never let anyone help. So, yes, never."

"Way to go, we saw you stop and talk to that woman. She was sitting at the table with the belly dancers," Matt said.

"Yeah, you should invite them to sit at our table," Kyle suggested.

"The one I was talking to, the gorgeous woman with the long black hair, was Sarina," Tony stated as if it should be common knowledge.

"Well, did you ask for her phone number?" Kyle asked.

"Hell no, she's already turned me down twice. Let's get out of here," Tony said.

"Don't look now but she's coming this way," Matt informed him.

"Tony, can I talk to you for a minute?" Sarina asked.

Tony saw her nervously rubbing her hands together and gave Matt and Kyle the look. They got up quickly and excused themselves. Sarina sat down.

"I think maybe we got off on the wrong foot the other day at the Renaissance Festival. If you're still interested, here is my number," Sarina said, and handed him her business card with her personal cell number written on the back. She stood to leave.

"I will call you," he said.

She gave him a huge smile and then walked back to her table where her friends were still seated.

～

"Well, guess this worked out for you, Tony." Kyle patted him on the back in jest, as Tony stared at the business card in his hand. "Way to go."

"Now you got her number, you better call her," Matt said.

"Why wouldn't he?" Kyle asked as if there couldn't be a reason not to call.

"I'll call her," Tony said. "Now, let's just leave it at that."

He got into his truck, and when Kyle tapped on the window Tony opened it.

"Not tonight, though, man. Stay tough!" Kyle coached him and walked away.

Driving home, Tony couldn't believe how badly he wanted to call her—like right then. But it would be just plain stupid and no way could he do it or he wouldn't stand a chance. He didn't want her to think he was desperate or too eager. The chemistry between them was strong and he wanted her. He was definitely taking a cold shower when he got home and waiting to call her until tomorrow.

CHAPTER 6

*D*ana picked up Kelsey and then Sarina in the morning and they were off to Emma Krumbee's Apple Orchard. It wasn't something they usually did, in fact it was something they hadn't ever done before, which was why they were doing it. Along with the apples, there was an arts and crafts fair and live music at the orchard this weekend. It would be a fun and interesting day, especially if they managed to actually make some apple pies later. She was excited. Now if she could just stop thinking about Tony and wondering when and *if* he would call.

They were walking through the arts and crafts tents when she heard her phone ring. Anxiously, she pulled it out of her purse to see who was calling. It was a number she didn't recognize which meant it potentially could be Tony. She immediately accepted the call.

"Sarina?" the voice said.

"Yes," she answered, while walking away from the tents and noise so she could hear better.

"It's Tony. Did I catch you at a bad time?" he asked.

"No, it's fine. I'm at an art fair and it's a bit noisy."

"I think we did get off to a bad start, so I was wondering if you'd like to go to the Renaissance Festival with me tomorrow, and maybe we could try this again? We can just walk around, check out the shops, try some of the foods and get to know each other." He paused, waiting for her answer.

"I'd love to," she answered enthusiastically.

"I can pick you up in my shiny new truck, if you're okay with that?" He couldn't stop the pride showing through in his voice.

"I do know a lot about you with all your loan information so I think it should be safe." She laughed. "I'll text you back my address. What time?"

"Is one o'clock okay?" he asked.

"Perfect. I'll be ready then," she answered.

"See you then," Tony said and ended the call.

Dana and Kelsey were standing off in the distance waiting for the call to end and then came over to where she was standing.

"Well?" Kelsey asked.

"It was Tony, and we're going to the Renaissance Festival tomorrow afternoon." She couldn't help smiling.

Tony pulled up promptly at one. Sarina was dressed in black shorts and a teal green gauzy flowing sleeveless top with a deep V- neck to show off her cleavage. Well, she wanted to keep him interested, right? She picked up her small, light-weight purse, one she could easily slip over her shoulder, and opened the door to see Tony's handsome, chiseled face smiling down at her. She locked the door to her townhouse hoping her rapid pulse wouldn't get the best of her as they walked out to his new silver Chevy Silverado.

On the way, they talked about his new truck, the weather

and the apple orchard. Sarina was nervous, but the simple conversation about everyday things put her at ease and soon they were inside the Renaissance Festival.

"What kind of food do you like?" Tony asked. "The festival is known for its unusual foods. Scottish Eggs, Turkey Legs, Popovers, Pickles on a Stick—."

"You seem to know a lot about the Renaissance Festival. Did you used to work out here?" she asked, extremely curious.

"No, but when I was in college, my friends and I made it a ritual to come every weekend, so I know this place pretty well. Of course, after college, I usually only made it out once a year except when I wasn't in Minnesota for a few years," Tony informed her.

"Did you make it a practice of trying to pick up women, out here?" she asked.

"Yes, as a matter of fact, only we weren't too good at it." He laughed. "Except for this year, but I don't think it really counts if you don't get a phone number."

"Probably not. But eventually you did! I am hungry, let's give the popovers a try."

The day went quickly and way too soon they were back at her townhouse with Tony walking her to the door. Sarina debated on inviting him in, but decided that was best left for another time. *Maybe the next time.*

"I had a really good time," Sarina said.

"Me, too. Would you be up to getting together again?"

"That would be nice." Sarina hoped she didn't sound too eager. It was a perfect, clear, moonlit night with a sky full of stars. She and Tony were only inches apart and he leaned in and kissed her gently on the lips. She felt like she was in heaven, and she definitely wanted more. But he was being the perfect gentleman and ended the kiss. He stepped back a little.

"I will call you tomorrow," he promised. "And I think maybe we'll have to make attending the Renaissance Festival every year *our thing*. This may just be the beginning of Sarina and Tony."

"I'd like that," she agreed. Standing in her doorway moments later, she watched Tony drive away and hoped she'd be seeing him a lot more in the future.

Sarina and Tony—she could get used to that.

Not the End, but the Beginning!

RECIPE

Easy One Bowl Apple Pie

½ Cup Butter (1 stick)
  1 Egg
  1 Cup Granulated Sugar
  1 tsp. Vanilla
  1 Cup Flour
  1 tsp. Baking Powder
  4 Large Apples Peeled and Sliced
  1 tsp. Cinnamon
Beat egg in medium sized bowl. Then add all remaining ingredients and mix well. Spread mixture in a greased 9-inch pie plate, sprinkle with cinnamon and bake for 1 hour at 350 degrees.

This recipe makes its own crust.

ABOUT THE AUTHOR

ROSE MARIE MEUWISSEN

Rose Marie Meuwissen, a first-generation Norwegian American born and raised in Minnesota, always tries to incorporate her Norwegian heritage into her writing. After receiving a BA in Marketing from Concordia University, a Masters in Creative Writing from Hamline University soon followed. Minnesota is still where she calls home.

She has traveled around the world, including Scandinavia, but still has many places to see, enjoys attending Scandinavian events, writing conferences and is usually busy writing Minnesota Lakes Contemporary Romances, Viking Time Travel Romances or Norwegian Traditions Children's Books.

Visit her at www.rosemariemeuwissen.com or www.realnorwegianseatlutefisk.com.

NOVELS:

- *Taking Chances*—a contemporary romance novel set in Minnesota and Arizona.
- *Married by Saturday*—a contemporary romance novel set in Minnesota and Montana.
- *Looking for Mr. Right*—a contemporary internet dating romance novel set on Prior Lake in Minnesota—*Coming soon!*

NOVELLAS:

- *Annika—A Christmas Romance*—a contemporary romance set in Minnesota with a Nordic theme during the Christmas Holidays.
- *Skol! Viking Blonde Ale*—a contemporary romance set in Minnesota at an Autumn festival complete with a fortune teller, ale and Vikings!
- *Choosing to Live*—a Norwegian woman's journey during WWII to survive the Nazi Occupation of Norway—*Coming soon!*

MINNESOTA LAKES ROMANCE NOVELETTES:

- *A Kiss Under the Northern Lights*—a Summer romance set in Ely, Minnesota on Big Lake.
- *Dancing in the Moonlight*—a Summer romance set in Malmo, Minnesota on Mille Lacs Lake.
- *Hot Summer Nights*—a Summer romance set in Prior Lake, Minnesota on Prior Lake.
- *Railroad Ties*—an Autumn romance set in Two Harbors, Minnesota on Lake Superior.
- *Blizzard of Love*—a Winter romance set in Lutsen, Minnesota on Lake Superior.
- *Nor-Way to Love*—a Spring romance set in Minneapolis, Minnesota on Lake Harriet.
- *Old Yule Log Fires*—a Christmas romance set in Excelsior, Minnesota on Lake Minnetonka.
- *A Date for Valentine's Day*—a Valentine romance set in Minnetonka Beach, Minnesota at the Lafayette Country Club on Lake Minnetonka.
- *Dance of Love*—a Fall Festival romance set at the Renaissance Fair in Shakopee, Minnesota.

CHILDREN'S BOOKS—REAL NORWEGIAN'S SERIES:

- *Real Norwegians Eat Lutefisk*—a Children's book about the tradition of Lutefisk presented in both English and Norwegian.
- *Real Norwegians Eat Rømmegrøt*—the second Children's book in the series about the tradition of Rømmegrøt presented in both English and Norwegian.
- *Real Norwegians Eat Lefse*—the third Children's book in the series about the tradition of Lefse presented in both English and Norwegian.
- *Real Norwegians Eat Krumkake*—the fourth Children's book in the series about the tradition of Krumkake presented in both English and Norwegian—*Coming next!*

MICRO-MINI NOVELETTE—COMING SOON!

- *Christmas Notes*—a collection of Christmas prose poems to warm the heart during the Christmas season.

CONTINUE READING A PREVIEW CHAPTER

Skol! Viking Blonde Ale

Fortunes, Love & Fate Series

By

Rose Marie Meuwissen

SKOL! VIKING BLONDE ALE

COPYRIGHT INFO

Print Edition
Copyright 2020 by Rose Marie Meuwissen

ISBN 978-0-9903788-3-9

Published in the United States of America
Nordic Publishing LLC
Cover Design by Raine English

SKOL! VIKING BLONDE ALE

FORTUNES, LOVE & FATE SERIES

Inga was living the dream, planning events for her own company, Unique Events, but she still hadn't found a guy who could be 'The One' for her. She never would've believed a fortune from a gypsy fortune teller promising her a 'love that surpasses time' could come true.

Erik moved from Norway to Minnesota to expand his Nordic Brewing company in the U. S. He'd promised himself to devote all his time to the business, but how was he to know that an unknown force of fate would introduce him to a woman he couldn't walk away from?

Their attraction could not be denied because ultimately, they were destined to be together. But could the Atlantic Ocean keep them apart? Would that even be possible if they were truly soul mates?

INGA'S FORTUNE:

Someone from your past will reappear in your life.
Your true soul mate.
With him, you will experience a love that surpasses time.

PROLOGUE

James J. Hill Days in Wayzata on Lake Minnetonka
September

*I*nga pulled into the back-parking lot of Main Street Books at six. She couldn't believe it wasn't later. Friday night rush hour traffic on the 494 Freeway was bumper to bumper all the way from Eden Prairie to Wayzata. The weather was still holding its summer like temps and true Minnesotans would never pass up a beautiful autumn weekend to go up North to their cabins one last time before winter arrived. Today was the James J. Hill Days celebration in Wayzata and the main street was packed with people as she made her way into the book store to find her *Romancing the Lakes of Minnesota* book club. This month instead of their regular meeting, they planned to enjoy walking around and checking out the celebration. Probably was a good call, she thought, since it would've been difficult to hold their meeting in the crowded book store and the activity outside would've been immensely distracting.

"Am I the last one to arrive?" Inga asked as she approached the book club group standing in front of the latest arrival shelf where the romance section was located.

"Bet the traffic was awful," Nora stated.

"Ready, to brave the crowds?" Katie asked.

"I'm hungry and thirsty, let's go!" Violet said.

Inga nodded in agreement and followed the group out the door to Main Street. They made their way down the street stopping at booths to look at the novelties for sale until finally, they stopped at the end of the street where the most unusual trailer was parked. The sign above the open door read, 'Fortune Teller'. It appeared to be Vintage, but these days they could make anything look old, even if it was new. Although, she had to admit, she'd never seen anything like it before, even though she'd been to many events. After all, she was an event planner. Intrigued was putting it mildly. Unfortunately, there was no stopping her curiosity. So, she entered the trailer.

"Come in, please," a very thickly accented voice beckoned from inside the trailer.

"Hello." Inga ducked and stepped into the trailer, taking in all the antiques and draped surroundings.

"Take a seat," the lady in gypsy like garb directed. "Let me see what your life has in store for you."

Inga didn't believe in fortune telling, at least she didn't think she did, but what could it possibly hurt to oblige the lady. It might be worth a laugh later, so she sat down on the partially pulled out chair at the table.

The fortune teller took the seat across from Inga and reached for her hand.

Slowly, Inga extended her hand. When their hands touched, Inga felt a strange sensation flow through her entire body, almost like a spark of electricity. It only lasted a few seconds and then was gone. She had no idea what it was or what caused it, but she finally relaxed.

The woman's face seemed deep in thought and completely fixated on her hand. "You are a very special lady. Very strong and independent. I see happiness in your future."

"Do you see a man?" Inga wasn't sure why'd she'd asked that particular question.

"Yes." The woman continued staring at her hand. "A very handsome man."

"Well, there certainly are enough good-looking men around. What I need is one that is interested in me long enough to stick around for a while."

"You have not met 'The One' yet."

"When? When will it happen? I'm getting really tired of waiting around for him."

"Soon."

"So, is that my fortune?"

"No." The woman hesitated, then picked up a piece of paper and wrote a few lines down on it. She handed it to Inga. "This is your fortune: *Someone from your past will reappear in your life. Your true soul mate. With him, you will experience a love that surpasses time.*"

"Great. But I'm sorry, I don't believe in magic."

"That's okay you don't have to believe. It will happen anyway."

Their eyes locked for a moment.

Inga got up to leave. "How much do I owe you?" Inga asked.

"For you, no charge. I've been waiting for you."

"I don't understand."

The fortune teller waived her hand in a shooing motion, indicating Inga was done and should leave.

As Inga stepped out of the trailer, Katie rushed up the steps. "My turn."

"So, what do you think? Is the Fortune Teller legit?" Violet asked.

"What kind of a question is that? Of course, it's not real. No one can tell another person what will happen in their future," Stephanie said.

"Care to share?" Nora asked.

Inga handed the piece of paper to Violet, who in turn handed it to Stephanie, who in turn handed it to Gwen and lastly to Nora.

"At least it's a good fortune. Let's hope it comes true," Stephanie said.

"Come on, you're not buying into this stuff, are you?" Inga shook her head.

Minutes later, Katie came down the trailer's steps, paper in hand grinning from ear to ear.

Violet practically ran to the steps to be next.

Each romance book club member shared their fortune while the next one took their turn. Being romantics at heart, they were all thrilled to find romance in their fortunes.

They continued strolling leisurely down the other side of the street where the craft brewery tents were located.

Inga spotted a tent with *Nordic Brewing* as the name. She selected it out of the five tents because of her love for all things Nordic and Viking. In fact, the Viking Ship logo caught her eye first. She walked up to the counter to see the menu more closely.

"What can I get you?"

Inga looked up quickly when she heard the strong Norwegian accented English and to her surprise saw almost a *'Thor'* look alike, only his blonde hair was shorter. He could very well be from Viking blood, she thought. *Tall, muscular, with a chiseled face. Have I just died and gone to Valhalla?*

"What can I get you?" he repeated smiling broadly at her.

"What would you suggest?" she managed to get out. "I've never tried your brand before."

"For you lovely lady, I'd suggest the Viking Blonde Ale."

"Sounds absolutely perfect."

He turned his broad toned back toward her stretching the black T-shirt taut against his muscles and filled a plastic souvenir cup with Valhalla printed on one side and a picture of a Viking on the other side.

Inga pulled a five-dollar bill from her purse and set it on the counter. He handed her the cup instead of setting it down and her fingers lightly brushed his in the process. *There it was again.* A shiver of sorts shimmied its way through her body.

"Thank you, hope you enjoy it," he said as he picked up the money to put in the cash register.

"Thanks, I'm sure I will," Inga said while her eyes lingered on this modern-day Viking man. She felt sad that she would most likely not ever see him again. *Oh well, one can only wish.* She turned and walked away spotting her friends up ahead at a different craft brewery tent.

www.ingramcontent.com/pod-product-compliance
Lightning Source LLC
Chambersburg PA
CBHW022054170626
46808CB00003B/1462